MEGA MASH-UP

Robots v Gorillas in the Desert

Nikalas Catlow
Tim Wesson

Draw your own adventure!

Mega Mash-Up: Robots v Gorillas in the Desert

Published in the UK in 2011 by Nosy Crow Ltd
Crow's Nest, 11 The Chandlery
50 Westminster Bridge Road
London, SE1 7QY, UK

Registered office: 85 Vincent Square, London, SW1P 2PF, UK

A CIP catalogue record for this book is available from the British Library

ISBN: 978 0 85763 008 7

This book needs

YOU!

What if ROBOTS and GORILLAS had a race in the **DESERT?** What if they got **SLIMED** by stinky SAND SLUGS on the way and had to grapple with famous WRESTLING SCORPIONS?

Who would win this **wacky Race?**

You'll have to finish the illustrations and find out...

Prepare to **LAUGH** while you doodle and SNIGGER while you read.

Introducing the Robots from Nanaville

Mega-Bite

Robotron

Gadget the Great

iBot

Multi-Tool

Introducing the Gorillas from Jungoil

Silverback Steve

Ape-Face

King Well-Hairy

Nobby Knuckles

Grappling Sam

You'll need these... DRAWING TOOLS

These are the 3 tools that Nikalas and Tim have used to create the artwork in this book.

Using different tools helps create great drawings

texture page
pen zigzags
crayon rubbing from lino floor
cross-hatching pencil
crayon rubbing from floor
pencil rubbing from wooden door
scribbly pencil
There are loads of ways you can add texture to your artwork. Here are a few examples
crayon rubbing from wall
pencil dashes
DRAWING TIP!
Turn to the back of the book for ideas on stuff you might want to draw in this adventure
pen circles

Get ready for a really sketchy adventure!

Pencils at the ready...

On your marks...

Let's draw!

Chapter 1
Yes, We Have No Bananas

The GORILLAS and the ROBOTS are two of the greatest ever civilizations.
The Gorillas live high above a giant oil pit in a tree city called JUNGOIL.
Finish the tree house
Banana skin pile
Draw a couple of rubber tyres?

Add woody texture
Add another tree house
HOORAY! A truck full of bananas has arrived from Nanaville
OIL
OIL
OIL
Finish shading the oil pit
OIL
Is there anything else in the oil pit?

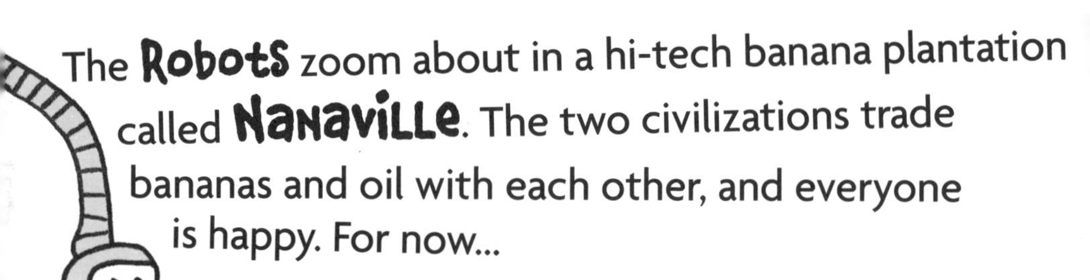

The **Robots** zoom about in a hi-tech banana plantation called **Nanaville**. The two civilizations trade bananas and oil with each other, and everyone is happy. For now...

This house needs windows
Add a Robot slipping on a banana skin
OIL STORE
Add more vents and pipes
Fill the crate with bananas

One day, the two leaders meet.
"Hello," says **King Well-Hairy**,
crushing **Gadget the Great** to his huge gorilla
chest in greeting. "**Hel-P!**" cries Gadget the Great,
Shocked. Sparks shoot out of his head, sending
10,000 volts of electricity up
King Well-Hairy's nose.

crush
bang
Add some electrifying sound effects
FIZZ!
FIZZ
Who else is getting shocked?!

The leaders **LIE FIZZLING IN THE DUST.**

AARCH!

Draw an onlooking Robot

Add some smouldering smoke

“You fried my nose. We’re not giving you any more oil,” splutters King Well-Hairy.

“You made me short-circuit. You can’t have any more bananas,” **bLeePS** Gadget the Great.

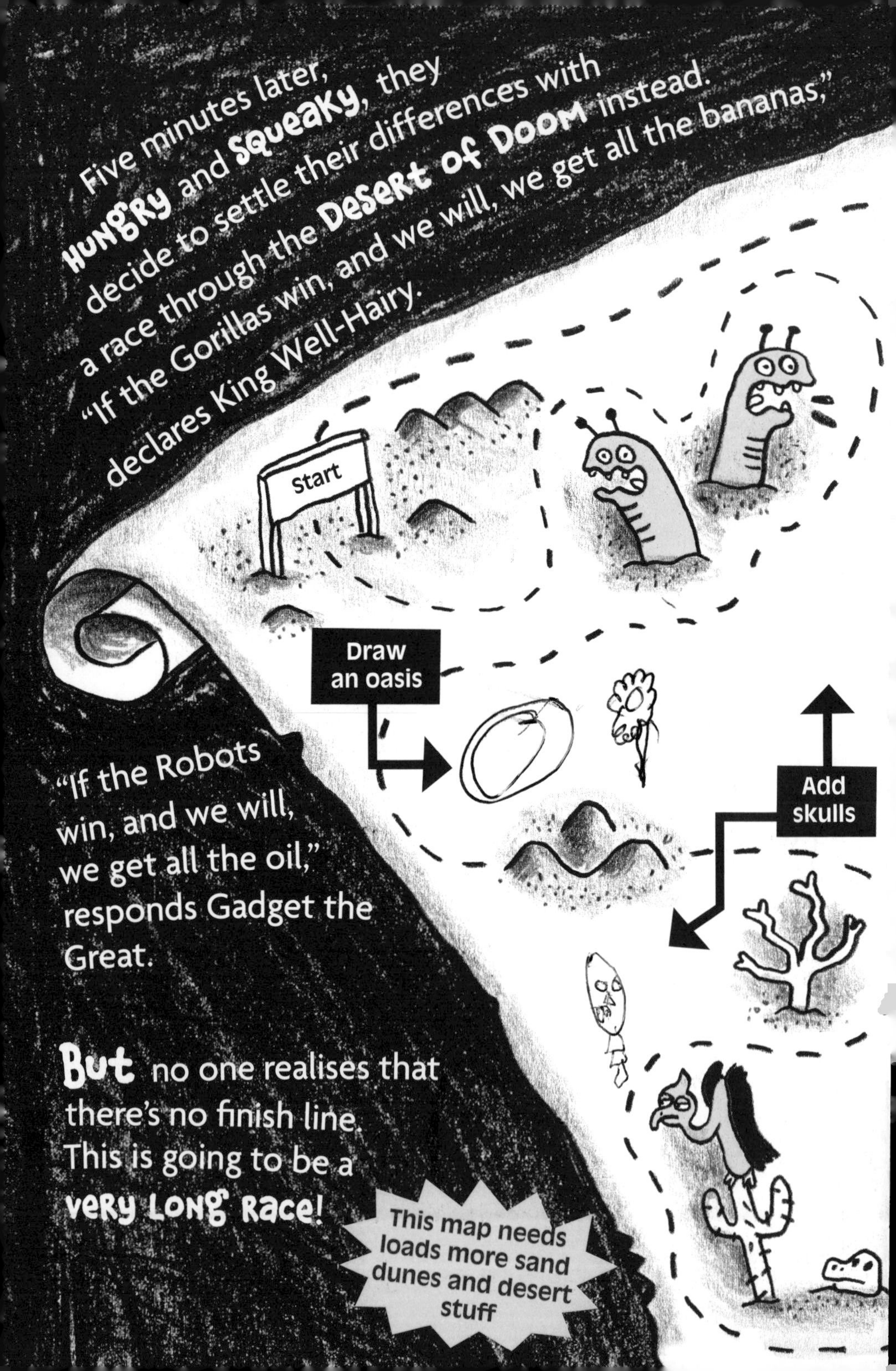

Five minutes later, HUNGRY and SQUEAKY, they decide to settle their differences with a race through the DESERT OF DOOM instead.
"If the Gorillas win, and we will, we get all the bananas," declares King Well-Hairy.
Start
Draw an oasis
Add skulls
"If the Robots win, and we will, we get all the oil," responds Gadget the Great.
But no one realises that there's no finish line. This is going to be a VERY LONG RACE!
This map needs loads more sand dunes and desert stuff

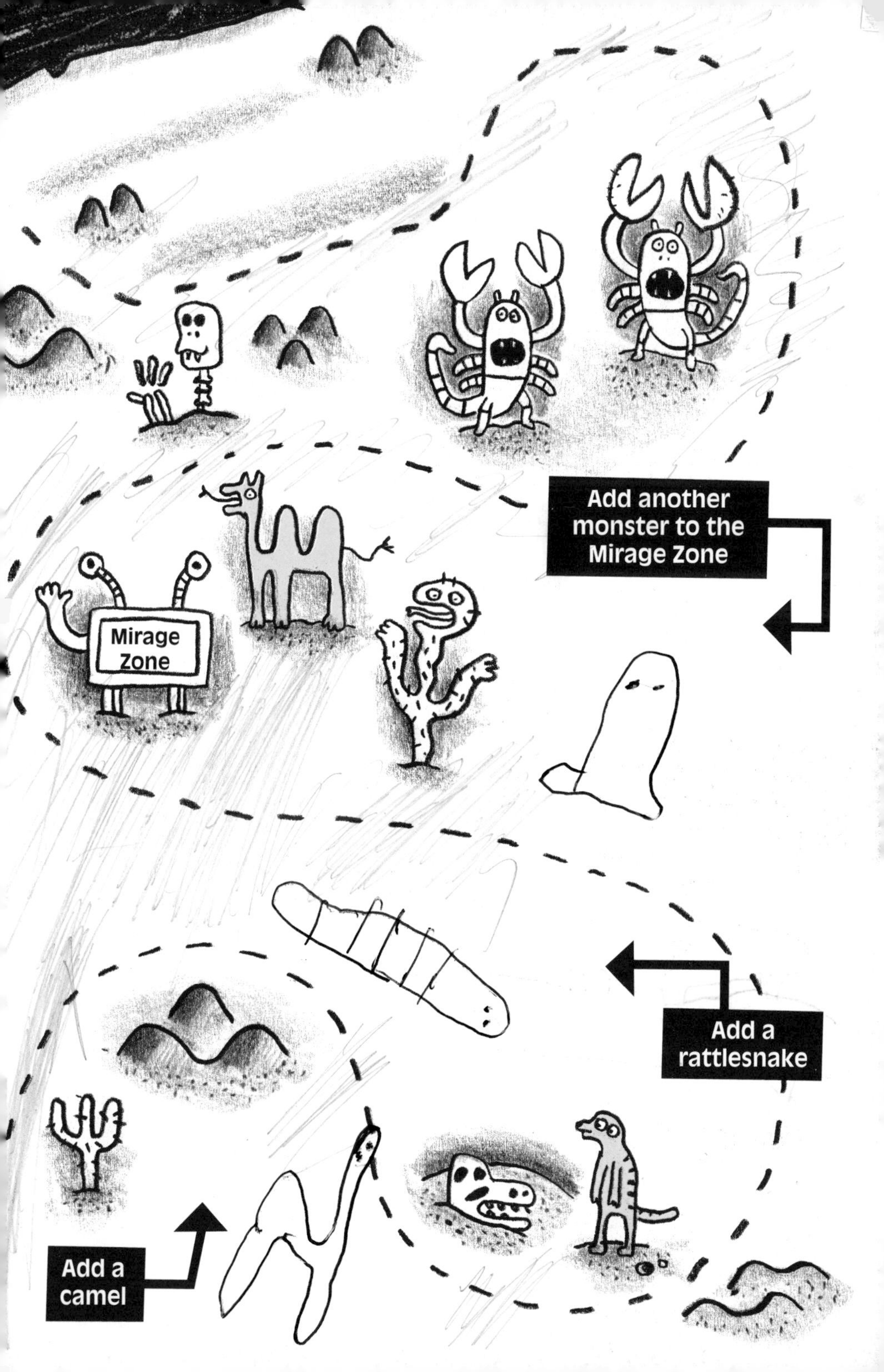
Add another monster to the Mirage Zone
Mirage Zone
Add a rattlesnake
Add a camel

The Robots are preparing for the race. "Let's use our cool **oil-firing bazookas** on those dumb Gorillas! Can't wait to see them fall on their hairy bottoms!" chortles Robotron.

Finish iBot's oil bazooka

Give Nanobot a heat-seeking oil bazooka

texture and colour the sand

Meanwhile the Gorillas are loading their **banana-firing tank suits** with ammo. “Those stupid Robots won’t know what’s hit ’em!” hoots Grappling Sam.

But the **Desert of Doom** isn't

called the **Desert of Doom** for nothing...

Chapter 2
Start Yer Engines

Start
Add START to the sign
Finish off Multi-Tool
Sam needs some hair

Gorillas and Robots jostle each other at the starting dune. "**Get Lost, Rusty!**" cries Nobby Knuckles. "**Eat bogeys, banana breath!**" shouts Bitomatic. And they're off!

Nine hundred and ninety nine years and six months, 15 days, 3 hours, 36 minutes and 48 seconds later, the race is **STILL GOING ON.**

"I want a yummy banana!" complains Nobby Knuckles. "You can't. **THEY'RE OUR AMMUNITION!**" snaps Grappling Sam.

MEANWHILE the Robots are so thirsty, they've started making **terrible clanking noises**.

"I'm seizing up," panics Mega-Bite. "My nuts and bolts are shrivelling."

GROAN
Smash
Draw a really thirsty-looking Robot leading the pack

It's time for some dirty tactics. "Help me turn this sign around," says Grappling Sam, chuckling hairily. "We'll send those rusty robots in completely the wrong direction and into this trap!"

What does a mega garlic burp look like?
Add other sound effects
Add more eyes and tentacles
What else is in the gooey pit?

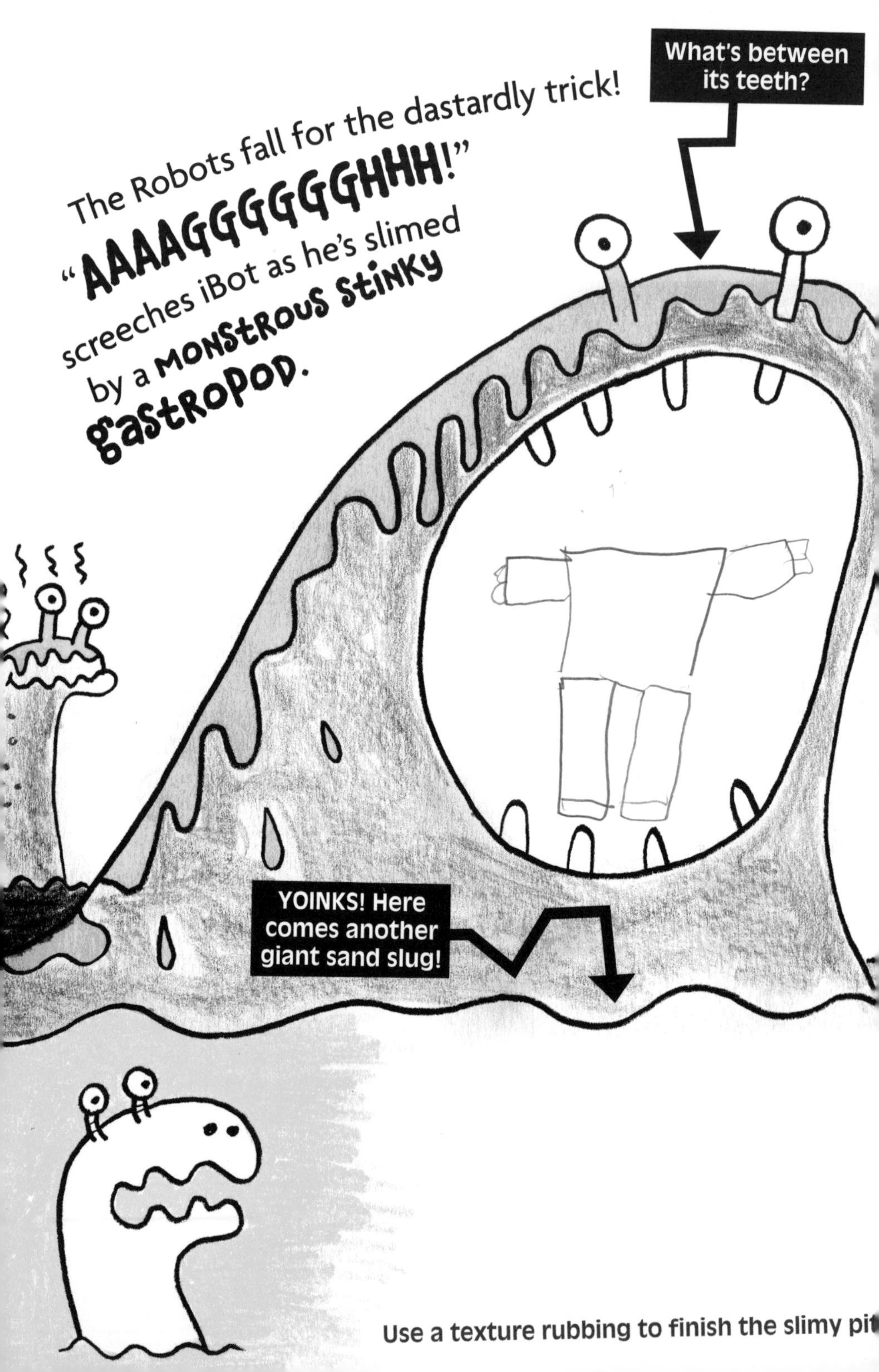
The Robots fall for the dastardly trick!
"AAAAGGGGGGHHH!"
screeches iBot as he's slimed
by a MONSTROUS STINKY
gastroPOD.
What's between its teeth?
YOINKS! Here comes another giant sand slug!
Use a texture rubbing to finish the slimy pit

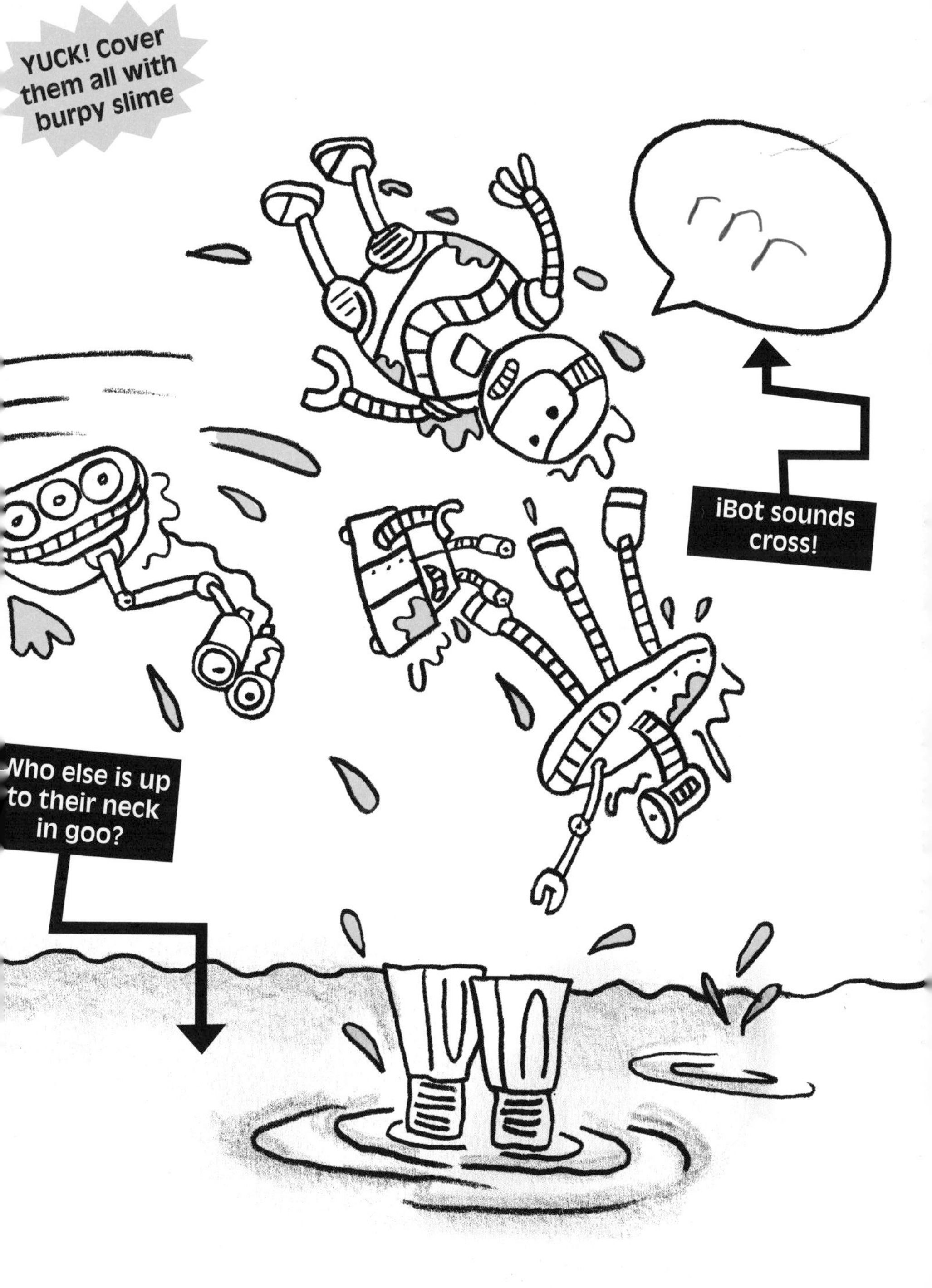

YUCK! Cover them all with burpy slime

iBot sounds cross!

Who else is up to their neck in goo?

The Robots slither slimily out of the sand slugs' **Stinky Pit**, to find they've overtaken the Gorillas! "It must've been a short cut!" cheers Mega-Bite.

"Revenge will be ours!" exclaims iBot. They build a fake banana bar – on **QUICKSAND**! "Those daft Gorillas'll do anything for a Bananamoccafrappuccino!"

"Oooh, oooh, oooh, make mine a large - aaahhh!" gibbers Nobby Knuckles, as he tumbles into the quicksand. The other Gorillas all pile in, and soon **they are sinking fast...**
Give the walls woody texture
OH NO! Fill the pit with sinking Gorillas

MENU
WE HAVE
NO
BANANAS
HA! HA! HA!
SIGNED
ROBOTS

The Gorillas haul themselves out of the quicksand and drag their knuckles on towards the **OASIS CHECKPOINT**.

Chapter 3
The Megawatt-BOT Plot

"I can't see any of those **WALKING DUSTBINS**. We must be in the lead!" cheers Ape-Face.

"Oooh! Look at that delicious bunch of bananas!" beams Nobby.

But suddenly a trap hidden by palm leaves flips up over his head. The Gorillas are trapped!

Draw more Gorillas in the trap
Texture the rock

"Mwa ha ha!" laugh the Robots, clanking out of hiding. "Now you will help us win the race, you overgrown monkeys. Who cares if we're seizing up, when you start running, your hairy legs will power our Megawatt-BOT and **VICTORY WILL BE OURS!"**

"You can't make us run!" protests Grappling Sam.
"Oh yes we can..." Robotron sniggers.
Who else is trapped in the wheel?

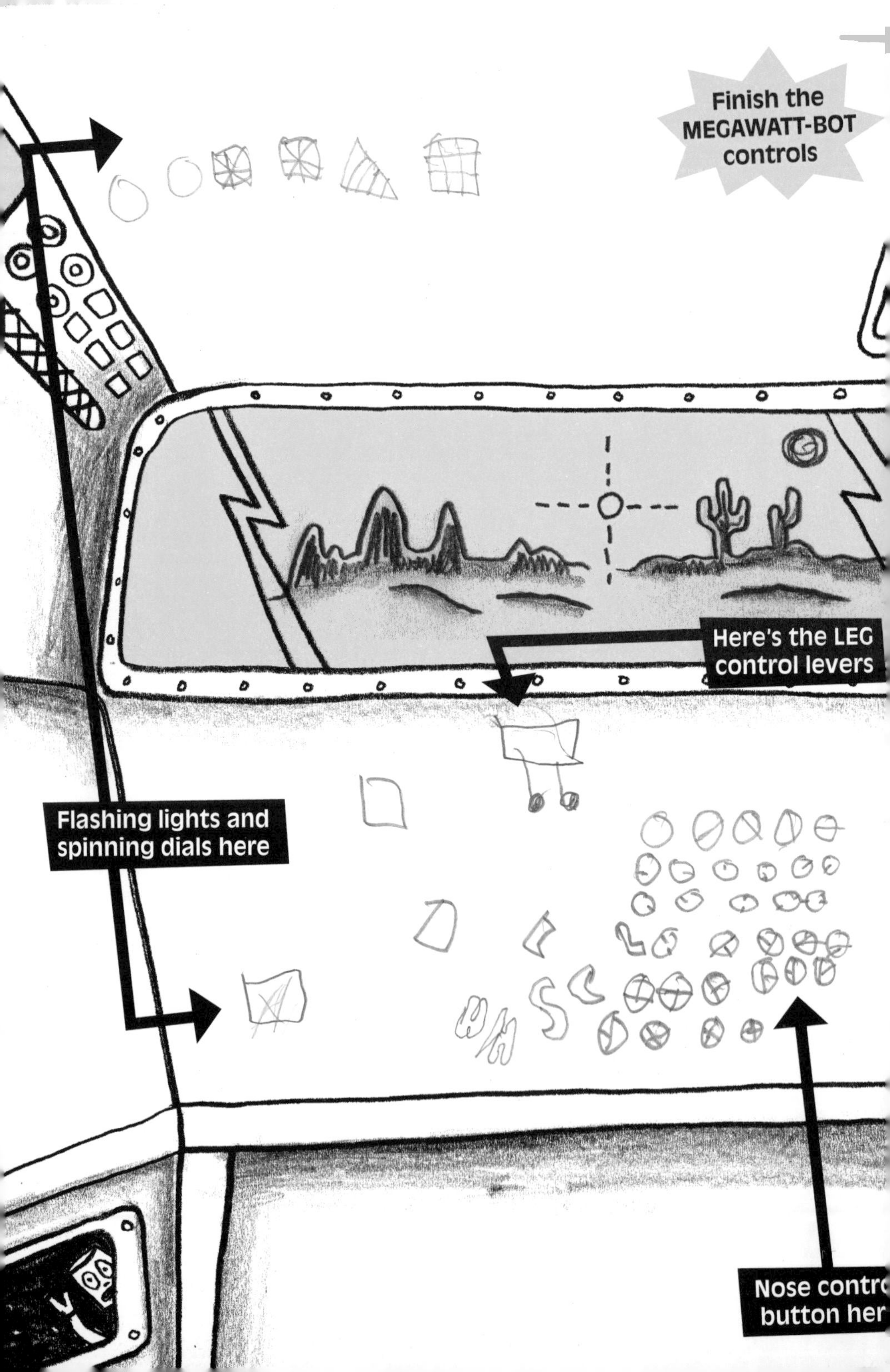
Finish the MEGAWATT-BOT controls
Here's the LEG control levers
Flashing lights and spinning dials here
Nose contr
button her

Multi-Tool starts fiddling with the Megawatt-BOT's control panel. "The resonating polarizing regulators and gravitational particle beam are ready!" he says. "Show-off," mutters Nobby Knuckles. "Setting the charge to **6000 VOLTS**!" cries Robotron.

A spark of electricity fizzes around the wheel. ZZZZZZZER-AP! "Hey! That tickles!" giggle the Gorillas, their legs moving faster than they've ever moved before. "It's working! It's working!" cry the Robots.

Who else is trapped and running?

Add more electricity flashes

Add more texture to the rock

Add more palm leaves

The **Megawatt-BOT** spins off into the desert, ploughing through the cactus forest and flattening everything in its way! The *Robots* are still cheering as they leave a path of devastation behind them...

Finish the cactus forest. Who else has got stuck?

Yikes! What are they shouting about?
What else has been flattened?

But seconds later, **CLATTER**, **CRUNCH**, the Megawatt-BOT ploughs into a stinky old camel pit, **DISINTEGRATING** into pieces!

What else is exploding out of the MEGAWATT-BOT crash!

Add a broken resonating polarizing regulator

Chapter 4
Do you See what I See?

Grappling Sam and Nobby Knuckles are flung from the wheel into the lead. "Look at that massive **banana ice-cream!**" drools Nobby, pointing greedily. "Hmmm," ponders Sam. "There's something funny about that banana..."

Mmmm! What does a giant banana sundae mirage look like?
MIRAGE ZONE

The fierce desert heat starts to play more tricks on the gullible Gorillas.

"**MONSTERS, MONSTERS** everywhere!" cries Nobby, diving out of sight.

"What monsters?" quizzes Grappling Sam.

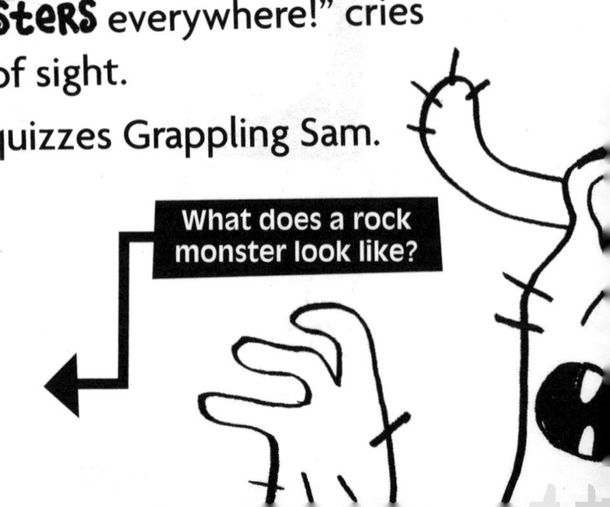

Ooh, what is so scary here?

Sam thinks he's wrestling with his old enemy, the Hairminator. Except he's not. "Oooh, oooh, oooh, you're going down," he chants.
"AAAAGGHHHHH!!" screams Sam, in sharp, needly pain.
Sam thinks a cactus looks like the Hairminator

What mirage is the camel looking at?
What's in this hole?
Texture the camel

Nobby Knuckles rubs **SAND FROM HIS EYES**.

"I keep thinking I can see Robots!" he says to Sam.

"**CURSE THESE WRETCHED MIRAGES!**"

"Those ARE Robots," points out Sam, pulling cactus needles out of his face. "They've caught up with us.

OUCH!"

Oh no! The Robots are getting ahead!

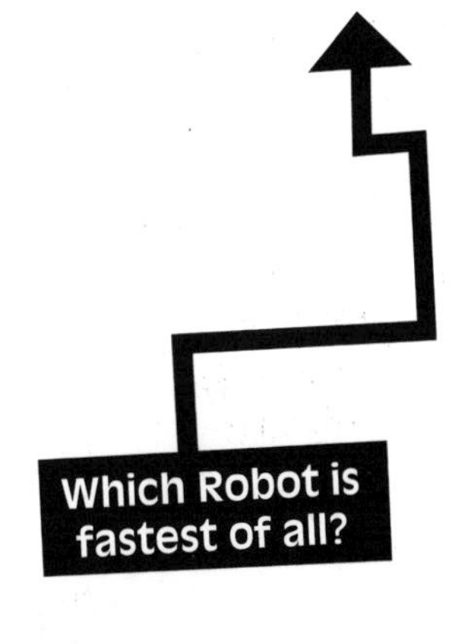
Which Robot is fastest of all?

Leaving the Mirage Zone behind them, they all race on towards **SCORPION TOWN**. "Could this be a place where giant scorpions meet and fight to the death, just for fun?" ponders Grappling Sam. They'll soon find out...

Chapter 5
Get Ready for Some Stinging Clenches!

Firing off bananas and oil at each other, the racers enter Scorpion Town. "**TAKE THAT, BANANA-BREATH!**" laughs Robotron as a stream of oil splats on to Grappling Sam's head. **GREASY!**

But someone is watching them...

Suddenly, two giant scorpions appear, in full wrestling kit. "I am King Sting!" says the first. "My killer speciality is the deadly tail swipe!" **SWOOSH, SWOOSH!**

"I am Clencher Claw!" says the other. "My killer speciality is a vice-like grip and squish!" SNAP, SNAP!

WOWEE!
What does Clencher Claw look like?

The racers are well shocked. “Quick! Let’s run away!” says Bitomatic. But Grappling Sam likes a bit of a wrestle. “**No, Let’s fight!**” he grins. What will they do?

Add Clencher Claw scowling back at Sam
Nobby sounds scared!

They decide to fight to the finish! **HURRAH!**
The Gorillas fire off their remaining bananas.
KAPOW! KER-CHUNK! King Sting swipes them away
with his tail. The Robots let rip with their BAZOOKAS.

Add fightin
sound effec

Everyone is fighting everyone!

It's not looking good for the Gorillas. But then, Grappling Sam pulls his old wrestling move, The Hook, on King Sting. **THE SCORPION GOES DOWN!** But Clencher Claw is still going strong...

Draw Clencher Claw bashing the Robots

Soup up the Loony Laser!

Loony Laser™

It needs more buttons and dials to work

Loony Laser operating instructions

"Let's use our **Secret weapon**!" laughs Robotron. "Activate the **Loony laser beam**, Robots!"

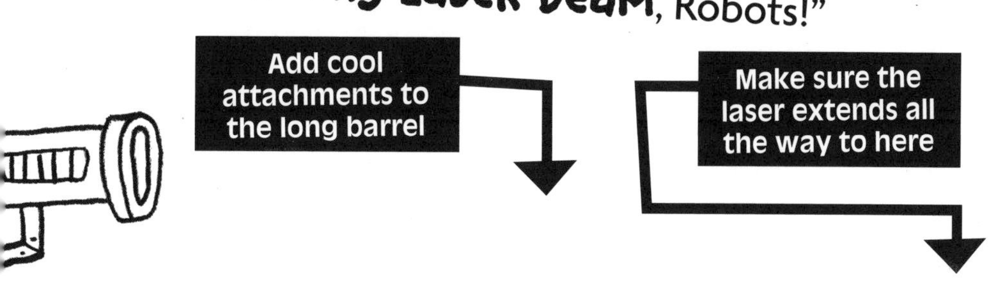

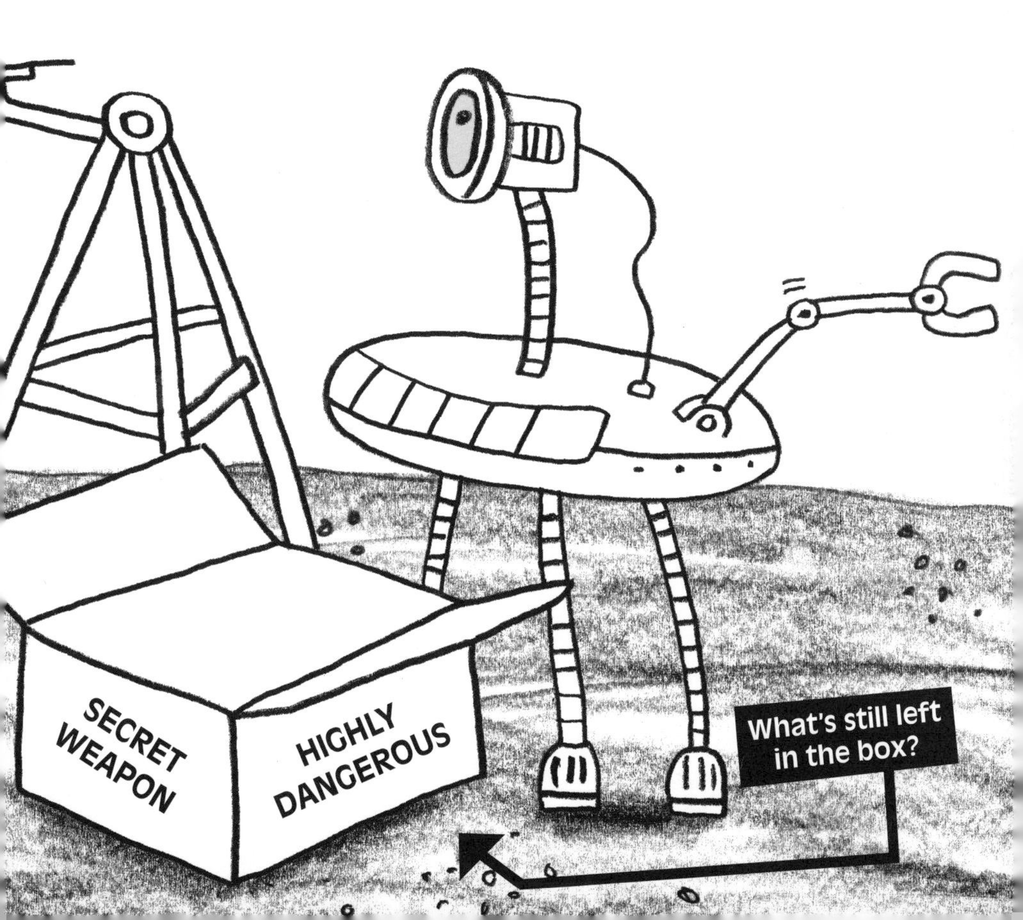

"I can't see where I'm aiming, my head is covered with mushy banana," complains Nanobot, firing off the loony laser willy nilly.
ZAP! ZAP! ZAP!
ZAP
Finish the laser. Don't forget to add buttons and dials

What do vapourized Scorpions look like
The laser VAPOURIZES the scorpions, then . . .

The Gorillas stagger around dizzily.
"I'm all singed," sniffs Ape-Face.
Add some dazed Robots
The Robots buzz about, looking the worse for wear. "My SPRockets are SMOKiNG," puffs Robotron.

Finish broken and battered Scorpion Town
FI
what's in in the laser crater?

All that's left of the nastiest wrestling giant scorpions in the world are two pairs of **SMOULDERING PANTS.** But the race must go on!

Chapter 6
Here We Go Again

Hungry and squeaky the Gorillas and Robots arrive at a familiar place. "**We're at the Starting Dune again**," protests Sam. "I think we've been going around in circles," adds Multi-Tool, dizzyingly.

Boy, does h
look angr

Everyone loo
puzzled

Finish the Mournful Mountains
What is Ape- Face saying on Live TV?

Add a barrel of bananas
Add another greedy Gorilla
Add shading to Jungoil

The Gorillas and Robots decide to call the race a draw. "**MMMMMM ... bananas...**" drools Nobby Knuckles as the Gorillas celebrate with an **all-you-can-eat Bananathon.**

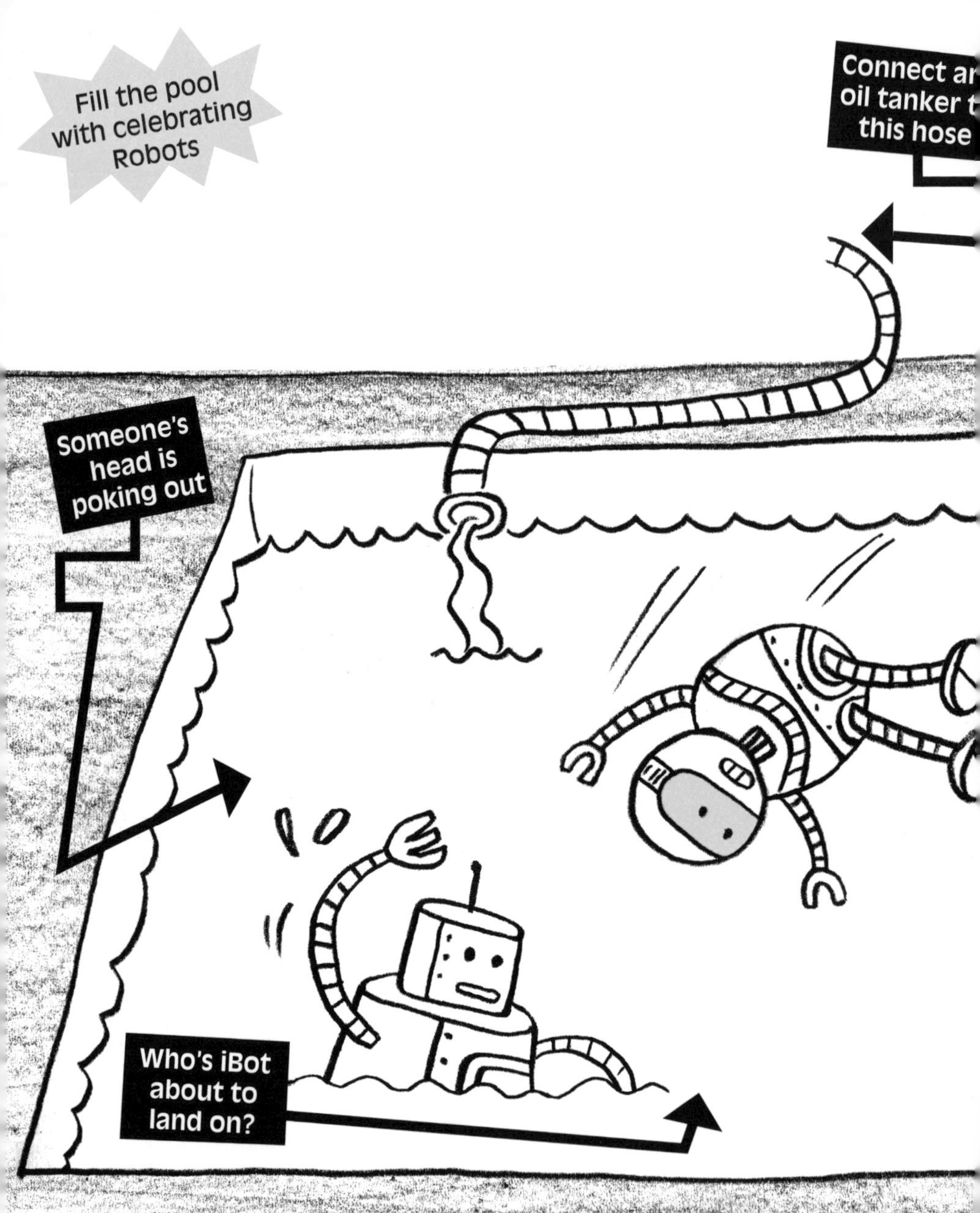

Back in Nanaville, the Robots are filling a swimming pool with oil. Robotron slips and falls head-first into the pool. "That's the stuff," he laughs. "**I'm well oiled**."

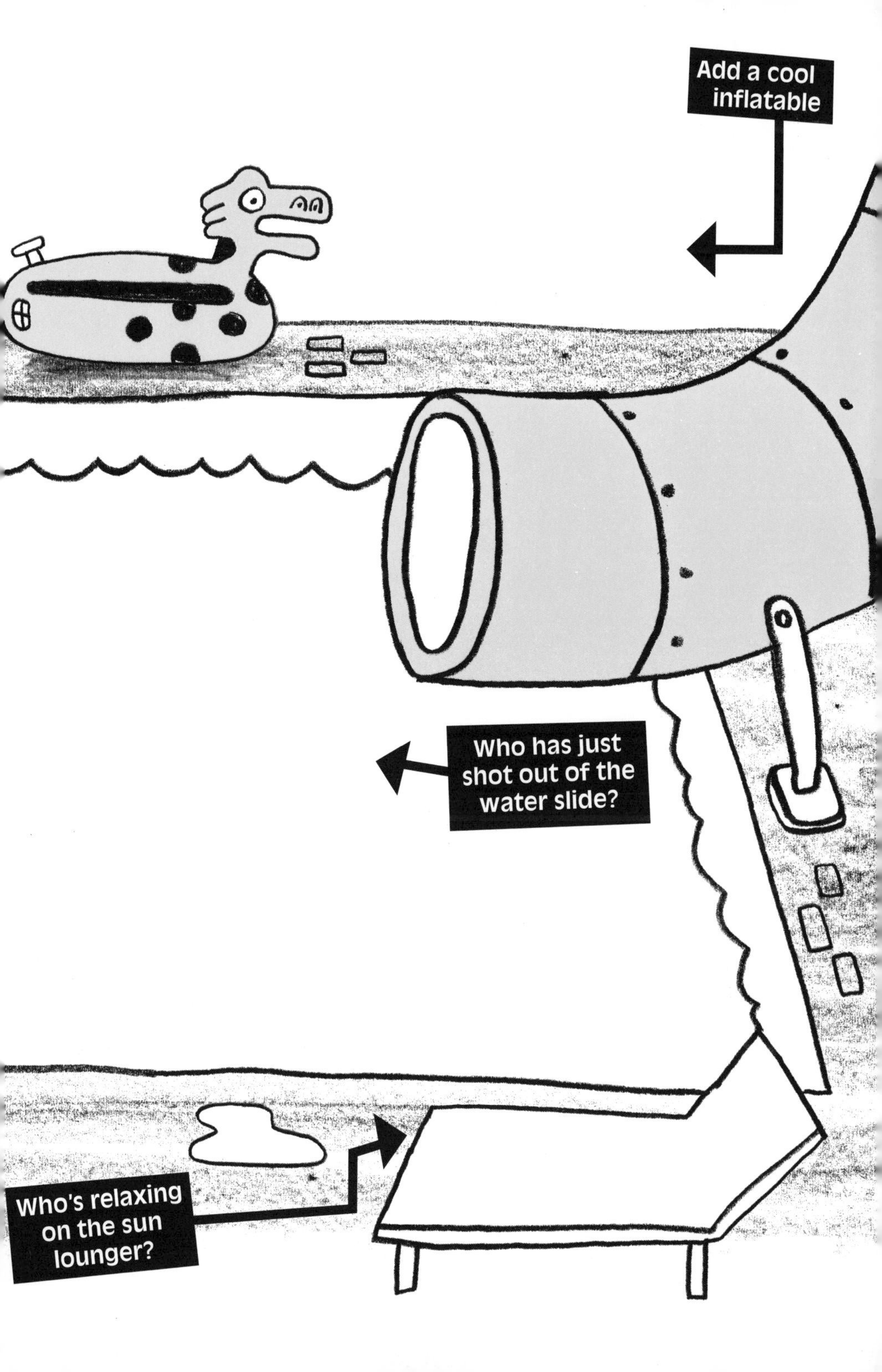
Add a cool inflatable
Who has just shot out of the water slide?
Who's relaxing on the sun lounger?

What's happening on the oil float?
OIL FOREVER
OIL FOREVER
DRUM!
OIL
OIL

The Gorillas and Robots celebrate their new-found friendship with a great Oil and Banana Festival.
Robotron and Rivet take centre stage in the Oil Drummers' Parade!
This lorry needs a driver and a passenger
Who else is celebrating in the parade?
POOP!
HONK!

"**OOOH! OOOH! OOOH!**" cry the Gorillas, as Grappling Sam and Nobby Knuckles pass by on their **Spectacular banana float**.

The two Gorillas fling bananas into the cheering crowd.
Finish the cheering Gorilla crowd!

During the closing ceremony there is a signing of **THE GREAT TREATY** between King Well-Hairy and Gadget the Great. "Hello," says King Well-Hairy, **CRUSHING** Gadget the Great to his huge gorilla chest in greeting. "**HEL-P!**" cries Gadget the Great, **SHOCKED**.

Sparks shoot out of his head, sending 10,000 volts of electricity up King Well-Hairy's nose. The two leaders lie **FIZZLING IN THE DUST**.

"OH NO, NOT AGAIN!" laugh the Gorillas and Robots. "If you think we're going to settle this with another 1000 YEAR
What do they remember most about the race?
iBot sounds exasperated!
What does Grappling Sam find funny?

race that never ends, then you've got another thing coming!" "CHORTLE, CHORTLE."

Picture glossary
If you get stuck or need ideas, then use these pages for reference.
SHERRIF'S OFFICE
TREE HOUSES
Single-storey
Multi-storey
SOUND EFFECTS
SPLAT
Ha Ha
WHACK
HOOT!
OIL SPLAT
OIL DRIP
If you like, you can copy the pictures. OR you can draw your own version.

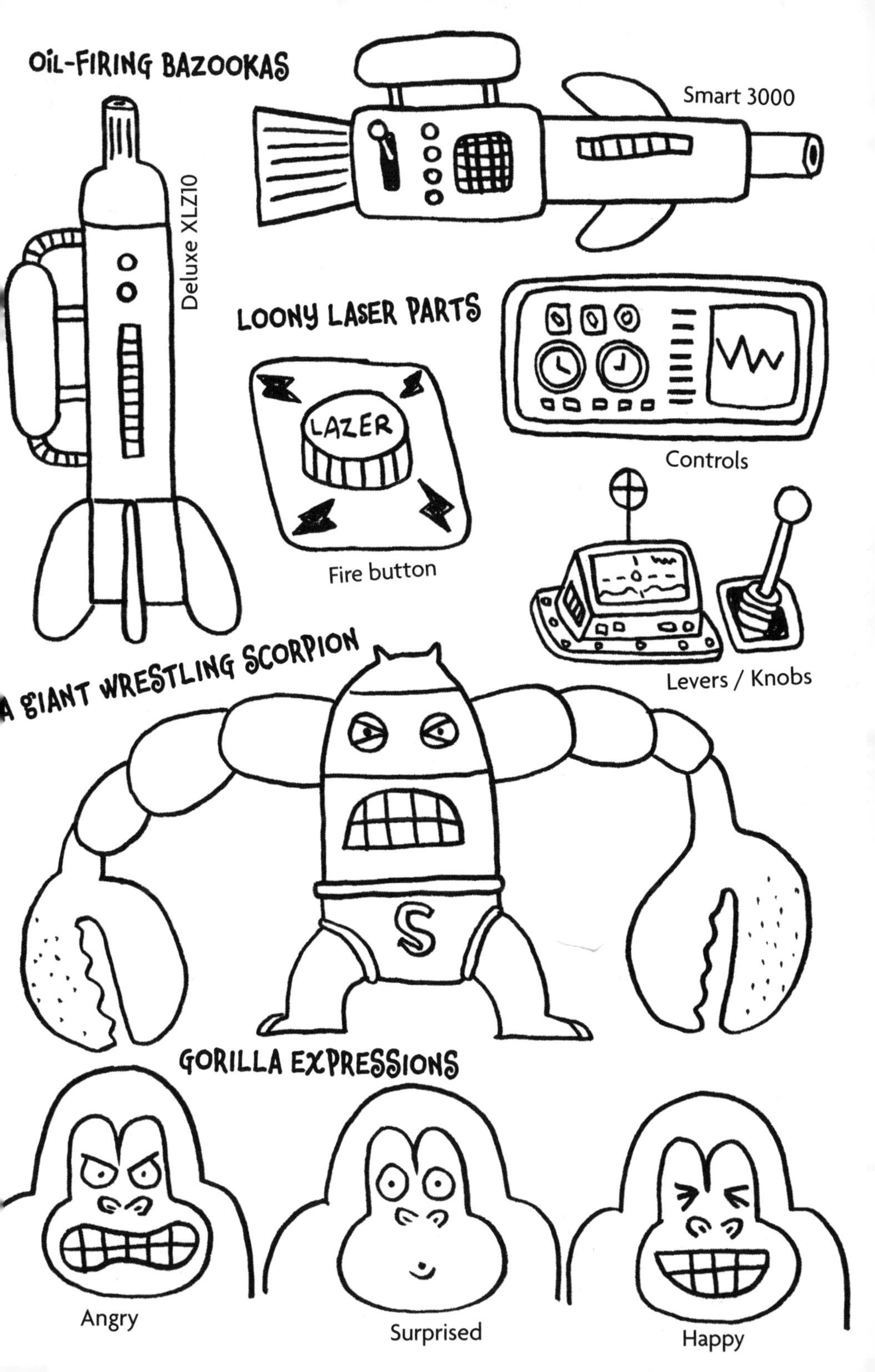
OIL-FIRING BAZOOKAS
Smart 3000
Deluxe XLZ10
LOONY LASER PARTS
LAZER
Fire button
Controls
Levers / Knobs
A GIANT WRESTLING SCORPION
S
GORILLA EXPRESSIONS
Angry
Surprised
Happy

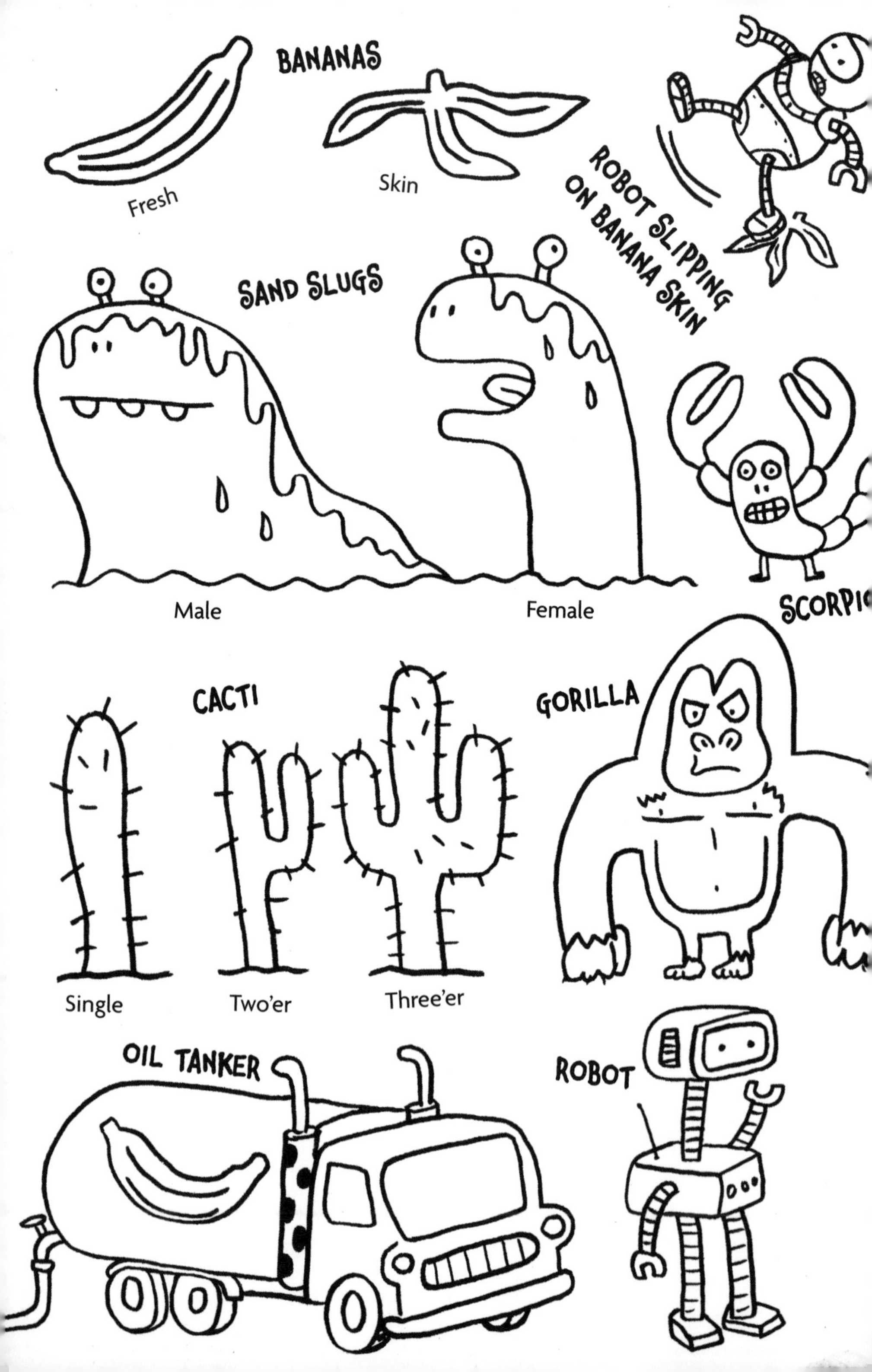
BANANAS
Fresh
Skin
ROBOT SLIPPING ON BANANA SKIN
SAND SLUGS
Male
Female
SCORPI
CACTI
Single
Two'er
Three'er
GORILLA
OIL TANKER
ROBOT